DUE DATE

THE MAGICAL MONKEY KING

Mischief in Heaven

Classic Chinese Tales Retold by
JI-LI JIANG

Illustrated by
HUI HUI SU-KENNEDY

HarperCollins*Publishers*

TO ALEX AND JUSTIN

Library of Congress Cataloging-in-Publication Data
Jiang, Ji-li.
The Magical Monkey King : mischief in heaven / adapted from the
classic Chinese tales by Ji-li Jiang ; illustrated by Hui Hui Su-Kennedy.
    p.   cm.
Summary: The Magical Monkey King attempts to achieve immortality the
easy way, gains god-like powers, and wreaks havoc in heaven.
    ISBN 0-06-029544-9 (lib. bdg.) — ISBN 0-06-442149-X (pbk.)
    [1. Folklore—China. 2. Monkeys—Folklore.] I. Su-Kennedy, Hui Hui,
ill. II. Title.
PZ8.1.J49 Ma 2002   2001039672
398.2'0951'045298—dc21   CIP
                                                                AC

Typography by Amy Ryan
1 2 3 4 5 6 7 8 9 10

First Edition

ACKNOWLEDGMENTS

I will always be greatly indebted to China for her long history and rich culture. Without China, I would be writing without roots.

This book has involved a lot of collaboration from Avi, the editor of Breakfast Serials; Ginee Seo, Susan Chang, and Stephen Fraser, editors at HarperCollins; and Vivian Xue, my closest friend for almost thirty years.

I would especially like to thank Kim Jensen, my personal editor as well as a good friend, who was directly involved in the crafting of this book from start to finish.

The story would not be the same without all of their valuable input.

AUTHOR'S NOTE

When I was a little girl growing up in China, Monkey King was my dear friend as well as my hero. All the children loved him—he was smart, brave, powerful, and mischievous. We were fascinated by the new challenges Monkey encountered, his struggle to beat the odds, the tricks he played, and his uncanny ability to always win. . . . There were so many stories about him, and every single one was filled with excitement.

Today, I am introducing our wonderful Monkey King to you. But this book contains only the first of many Monkey King tales. If you fall in love with him, I will tell you more stories about him. I promise.

Welcome to the world of the Magical Monkey King!

CONTENTS

STONE MONKEY IS BORN

Thousands of years ago in China, in the province of Ao-lai, there stood a towering mountain—the Mountain of Flowers and Fruits. At the very top of this mountain, perfectly balanced on its peak, was a rock as big as a castle. It was half hidden by a mysterious mist.

One night a furious storm exploded over the mountain. Never had there been such a storm! Bolts of lightning streaked across the sky. Thunder crashed and howled. Torrents of rain pelted the mountainside, and the animals living there fled in terror.

Suddenly, there was an earth-shattering blast. *Craaaack!*

The huge rock on the mountaintop split apart and fell to pieces thousands of feet below. All that was left on the peak was a black stone egg.

Strangely enough, as soon as the stone egg appeared, the storm ended. The air became calm and peaceful.

The sun rose and set. The rains fell, and the skies cleared. Ninety-nine days passed. And the stone egg remained motionless upon the mountaintop.

On the ninety-ninth night a gust of wind in the shape of a dragon descended upon the mountain. *Whoosh!* The dragon breathed fire onto the stone egg. At once it erupted into flame. Howling and roaring, the fireball grew until it was the size of an elephant.

For nine days and nine nights, the egg burned and burned. On the tenth day the fire died out. The egg, too, was gone. In its place—on the very top of the mountain—stood a small stone monkey.

The next day, a gentle breeze came and tickled the stone monkey. And when it did, the monkey's eyes began to twinkle! Then a soft rain came and washed him, and his stone skin changed into silky, golden fur. The sun came out and shone its warmth

upon the monkey, and he began to breathe. Slowly he turned his head from side to side. He stretched his arms and legs and wiggled his fingers and toes. And then, suddenly, he jumped into the air, rolled into a perfect somersault—and landed on his feet!

Monkey knelt down and bowed his head to the ground four times: to the east, to the south, to the west, and finally to the north. At last he lifted his head up toward the sky— and laughed! It was a long, mischievous laugh, loud enough to shake the tall trees to their roots and cause the earth to tremble.

And most amazing of all, as Monkey laughed, a beam of light shot out from his eyes and went straight up to Heaven.

Far above the sky, near the North Star, Jade Emperor, Ruler of Heaven and Earth, sat on his throne in the Cloud Palace. He was busy meeting with his ministers about the state of the universe when he was rudely inter- rupted. A shaft of light burst out of nowhere and filled the throne room. Neither Jade Emperor nor his ministers had ever seen such a thing before, not in Heaven nor on Earth.

Jade Emperor did not like mysteries. After all, he was the ruler of the universe! He turned to his two captains, Thousand-League Eye, who could see as far as a thousand leagues, and Thousand-League Ear, who could hear anything as far as a thousand leagues.

"Go find out what this strange light is and where it comes from," Jade Emperor commanded.

The two captains dashed away to the southern gate of Heaven, where they could look down on Earth. In the blink of an eye, they returned.

"Your Majesty," said Thousand-League Eye, "the light is coming from the tallest mountain in the province of Ao-lai. And when I looked more closely at it I saw . . . a little monkey."

"A little monkey?" exclaimed Jade Emperor. "Nonsense! How could a little monkey send a beam of light all the way to Heaven?"

Thousand-League Ear bowed. "We can't explain it, Your Majesty," he said, "but when I listened I could hear that monkey all the way up here. And he was laughing."

Jade Emperor leaned back in his throne and stroked his long gray beard. "Well, well," he said at last, "if it is just a little monkey, there is nothing for us to worry about."

Which only goes to show that even Jade Emperor can be wrong.

2

MONKEY ACCEPTS A CHALLENGE

For many years, a great clan of monkeys lived on the Mountain of Flowers and Fruits. They enjoyed a carefree life, swinging from the trees and playing in the streams. Whenever they were hungry, they gathered delicious fruit from the trees. Whenever they were thirsty, they drank crystal water from the streams. Life was easy and wonderful.

But when that furious storm came to the Mountain of Flowers and Fruits, it destroyed all the trees on the mountain. Day after day, the monkeys crept among the broken trees, searching in vain for something to eat.

One hot morning the hungry monkeys were sitting forlornly by a stream. "I wonder," said one monkey, who was more curious than the rest, "what would happen if we followed this stream up the mountain. We might find a place that was better than this one."

"Yes, yes," the other monkeys agreed. "It certainly can't be worse."

So they followed the stream as it wound through valleys and up steep cliffs. By late afternoon they had neared the top of the mountain and were feeling very tired. But they pushed on, past one more curve in the stream. As they came around the bend they found themselves at the bottom of a gigantic waterfall, an immense white curtain of rushing water casting down billions of water pearls, each one glittering in the sunlight.

"Ohhhh, how lovely!" said the monkeys, clapping their hands in delight.

The waterfall was so high that they could not see the top, so wide that all the monkeys holding hands could not reach from side to side, so dense that not even the sharpest-eyed monkey could see through it.

"If this waterfall is so beautiful on this side," the curious money wondered, "what do you think lies on the other side?"

The monkeys looked at each other, but no one answered.

"Who will dare to go and look?" asked the curious monkey.

"Not me!" answered one monkey. "I'd get soaked!"

"Or crushed by the water!" said another.

"Worse! You'd drown and be swept away by the mighty current!" others cried.

All the monkeys whined and made excuses.

The curious monkey leaped upon a tree and shouted out, "I have an idea. Whoever is brave enough to go through the waterfall and discover what is on the other side will become our *king*! What do you say to that?"

"Very good," said an old gray-haired monkey who was grandmother to the clan. "But I don't think there is anyone foolish enough to accept the dare."

"Who will go? Who will go?" the monkeys jabbered. Though they pushed and shoved each other, no one had the courage to step forward.

Suddenly, a loud voice boomed, "I will go!"

Standing on a rock hundreds of feet away was a monkey the clan had never seen before. He was small; his fur was silky and golden in color. And his eyes were shining with a strange light.

"Who are you? And where do you come from?" asked the curious monkey.

"I am Stone Monkey, born of Heaven and Earth," Stone Monkey said. "I'm so brave, I'll do anything."

"Bragging! Bragging!" the other monkeys jeered, making faces at this new monkey.

Monkey did not say a word. He just laughed. Then he jumped. He jumped higher than the highest tree in the forest, somersaulted, and landed on his feet right in front of the astonished monkeys.

"Did you say I was bragging?" he asked. "Well, then, if I go through the waterfall, will you truly make me your king?"

Grandmother Monkey walked out of the crowd and looked into Monkey's eyes. They were the strangest eyes she had ever seen. "Are you really so foolish as to try?" she asked.

Monkey craned his neck, pretending to search among the crowd. "Well, I don't see anyone else volunteering," he said. He

stretched out his arm and bowed deeply. "But if any one of you is brave enough, please be my guest."

"Oh, you boastful monkey," several monkeys cried out. "Shame on you!"

"Silence!" ordered Grandmother Monkey. She turned back to Monkey. "Very well," she said. "Let's see if you really are as brave as you say."

"If I succeed, don't forget what you have promised." Monkey winked at the curious monkey.

"Go! Go!" the monkeys chanted. "You'll see. You'll never come out alive!"

Monkey scampered through the crowd until he reached the edge of the giant waterfall. The rushing water made a noise like thunder. Very slowly he stretched out his legs and his arms. He turned his neck back and forth and wiggled his tail.

In awed silence, the monkey clan watched.

Monkey crouched down, closed his eyes, took a deep breath—and leaped straight into the waterfall—and vanished.

3

MONKEY BEHIND
THE WATERFALL

Monkey burst through the waterfall and landed on his feet. He opened his eyes and found himself in a vast cave illuminated by soft light.

Everywhere he looked, he saw gardens and streams. Clusters of nuts and fruit—including pink peaches, his favorite food—hung from thousands of flowering trees. Multicolored birds flew through the air, singing songs that filled his heart with joy. "Oh my," murmured Monkey. "This is a hidden paradise. And it was I who discovered it."

After crossing over a beautiful iron bridge bathed in warm light, he came to the edge of one of the gardens. There he spied a gateway covered with flowering vines. Monkey passed through it and found himself in a wide chamber. And he paused, amazed.

There were tables and chairs, dishes and cups, beds and couches, all carved out of the finest pale-green marble, all ready to be used. There were blankets spun from the softest silk. There were books, full of pictures that seemed to come alive when he glanced at them. There was even a throne covered with glittering jewels.

"What is this place?" Monkey wondered as he explored room after room. Eventually he found himself outside again. It was then that he noticed the inscription etched in the marble over the gateway:

This Blessed Cave of the Water Curtain Leads to Heaven!

"Leads to Heaven!" Monkey exclaimed, overcome with joy. "Tcha! This palace must be meant for me. After all, I am the Stone Monkey, born of Heaven and Earth. This is my kingdom, for I am now the King of the Monkey Clan!"

Monkey leaped up, did a little dance, somersaulted four times, then ran back to the waterfall as fast as he could.

Meanwhile, on the other side of the waterfall, the monkey clan waited anxiously. As time passed, they became convinced that the bragging monkey had indeed drowned.

"Serves him right," said one.

"It's too bad," said another, shaking his head. "If only he had not been so arrogant. . . . Oh! What's that?"

A golden shadow darted out of the curtain of water and flew over their heads. It rolled into a perfect somersault and landed right behind them. The entire monkey clan shouted. It was Monkey!

The monkey clan crowded around him. "Is the water very deep? Did you see anything interesting? What's it like on the other side?"

"Ah, my friends, you would not believe it," Monkey began. "I found—" He paused slyly.

"What? What? What did you see?" The monkeys begged him to continue.

Monkey burst into laughter. "I found a paradise for all of us. Come with me!"

And so the monkey clan put aside their fear and followed Monkey to the thundering waterfall. One by one they crouched—just as he had done—closed their eyes, and jumped straight through the water.

"My goodness!" they all cried when they came out on the other side. Looking this way and that, they rushed across the iron bridge. Now screaming and laughing with excitement, they reached the vine-covered gateway and the green marble palace. Once inside, they snatched up dishes and cups, and fought to get into the beds. They climbed on top of each other, pushing, shoving, and squabbling gleefully.

"Fellow monkeys!" called a booming voice. They all turned around. There was Monkey, sitting on the jeweled throne, looking very serious.

"Well, what do you think?" he asked.

"It is beautiful! Wonderful! We are so lucky," the monkeys said.

"Words are as good as gold," Monkey said. "You made a promise that whoever was brave enough to go through the waterfall would be your king. Now what do you say?"

"Our king! Our king!" The monkeys

began to cheer. Old and young, male and female, they all knelt down, shouting, "Long live our Monkey King!"

"Wait, wait!" the curious monkey cried. "Our king is so amazing and brave. I think we should call him Magnificent Monkey King!"

"Long live Magnificent Monkey King!" The voices of thousands of monkeys now echoed through the stone palace and gardens.

As for Magnificent Monkey King, he laughed as he had never laughed before, just thinking of all the things he might now do.

4

MONKEY GOES SEARCHING

Year after year, Magnificent Monkey King and his monkey clan enjoyed carefree lives in the Cave of the Water Curtain. They spent their days in perfect happiness, swinging from vines and trees, eating fruits, and playing all sorts of monkey games. It now seemed that they would be happy forever in their new home.

But one day, something changed. It was during a birthday party for the king. All the monkeys had brought him beautiful flowers and delicious fruits—especially peaches, his favorite. Sitting on his jeweled throne, surrounded by his beloved monkeys, Monkey should have had the happiest day of his life. Instead, in the middle of the celebration, he burst into tears.

The monkeys were shocked. They had

never seen their king sad before. And now he was crying!

It was the curious monkey who stood up and said, "What is wrong?"

Monkey wiped away his tears. "Dear monkeys, we are happy today, but with each birthday we grow older and older. I just realized that one day we shall all die, and our joy shall end." He cried even harder.

The monkeys thought about what he had said. They hung their heads and started to cry, too.

Grandmother Monkey stood up. "Magnificent King," she said, "if that is what is making you sad, I have an idea. I learned from my grandmother, who learned from her grandmother, that there are three types of beings who never die. Why don't you go and learn their secrets?"

Monkey jumped up on his throne. "Who are these three types of beings?"

"First are the sages. They are the wise teachers. They *study* the secret of life and learn to stay young forever. Second are the immortals, like Jade Emperor, who *know* the secret of life and so can live forever. Finally there are the Buddhas, such as the great Buddha and Goddess Guan-yin. Since they have achieved complete enlightenment, they *live* the secret of life."

Monkey was so excited that he did a somersault in the air. "What a brilliant idea, Grandmother," he said. "I will seek out a sage and learn the secret of living forever. Then I'll come back and teach it to all of you so we can enjoy our lives together forever."

Monkey was so enthusiastic that he said his goodbyes immediately. Before an hour had passed, he started off in search of a sage who could teach him the secret of eternal life.

Monkey traveled hundreds of leagues to countless far-off lands. He met with people of all sorts. He even learned to dress and speak like them, but in all of his travels he discovered that most people were more interested in money and fame than in the secret of life. Even after nine years of searching, not a single worthy sage did he find. He was beginning to think he would never find one.

Then, one day, he was walking in a deep, dark forest far from the Mountain of Flowers and Fruits. Here the leaves were so thick that no sunlight came through. A peaceful silence filled the air.

In the middle of this forest he heard a man singing:

I chase no glory, I pursue no coin.
Fame and wealth are passing clouds to me.
A simple life prolongs my days.
And those I meet upon my way
Are sages one and all,
Are sages one and all.

"At last!" cried Monkey. "I have found a sage!" He ran toward the sound of the voice.

A man was cutting branches from the trees.

"Revered sage," Monkey cried, bowing deeply. "Consider me your student."

At these words the woodcutter looked up, astonished, and dropped his axe. "But I am not a sage, sir," he said. "I'm just a

humble woodcutter. You mustn't bow to me."

"If you are not a sage, why did you sing that song?" demanded Monkey.

The woodcutter looked alarmed. "I—I didn't intend to mislead anyone," he stammered. "That song was taught to me by a great sage who lives over the hills from here."

"What is his name?"

"Master Subhodi."

Monkey grinned. "Well, well. Then you must show me where this sage lives."

The woodcutter, who was a little frightened of Monkey, led the way along a path in the woods. It grew darker and darker. When it grew too dark to see, the woodcutter stopped. "I can go no farther," he said. "Follow this path over nine hills and nine streams, and you will come to Master Subhodi's cave."

The forest was pitch-black, but Monkey was untroubled. His bright eyes lit the way for him. Monkey followed the path up the hills and across the streams, just as the woodcutter told him. After a day of walking, the forest grew a little less dark, and by the second day it was lighter still. At last Monkey came to a cave with huge stone doors. He tried them, but they were locked.

As Monkey King stood there, a prickling sensation came over him. He felt that something strange was about to happen. Nervously, he jumped into a tree. The whole world grew still. The only sound Monkey heard was the beating of his own heart.

Then he heard a noise. *Crreeeeaak!* Slowly, very slowly, the great stone doors began to swing open.

5

MONKEY MEETS A SAGE

A tiny child dressed in filmy white silk emerged. Peering this way and that, she called out in a silvery voice, "Where is the one who came to see Master Subhodi?"

Monkey King, looking down from the tree, was too frightened to answer.

The child looked around again. This time she shouted: "Is there anyone here who was *born from a stone?*"

Monkey was so startled that he almost fell out of the tree. He leaped to the ground and said, "Little one, I was born from a stone."

The tiny child gazed fondly at Monkey. "You naughty monkey! Hiding in a tree," she scolded. She reached up, grabbed some of his golden fur, and pulled. "Hurry now. Master is waiting for you."

"Are you sure it's me he's waiting for?" Monkey asked, truly astonished. "Ow!"

The child was still tugging at his fur. "Did you come from a faraway mountain?" she asked. "Are you here to study how to live forever?"

"That's me," Monkey said with delight. "Truly, your master must be wise—ouch!— if he already knows who I am."

"Master Subhodi knows everything. Now come along," the child said.

Monkey followed the child into the cave, which smelled of burning incense and was filled with a soft blue light.

After they had walked along for about a hundred paces, the tiny child disappeared. Monkey found himself in a room that held a large wooden platform that gave off a delicate perfume. Around the platform, sitting on mats, were thirty or so students. And upon the platform, sitting as still as a statue, with his legs crossed, was Master Subhodi himself.

Master Subhodi's long beard and eyebrows were snowy white. His round face was kind, and his eyes gleamed with knowledge and wisdom. Everything about him was solemn and dignified.

"MASTER!" shouted Monkey, shattering the silence of the cave and startling several students as he made a clumsy bow before the sage. "I OFFER YOU MY MOST HUMBLE RESPECTS!"

"Where are you from?" the master asked, unruffled. His voice was soft but resonant.

Hoping to impress him, Monkey replied, "I am from the great Mountain of Flowers and Fruits in the glorious province of Ao-lai. I was born from a huge stone atop that mountain. I am the Magnificent King of the Monkey Clan."

A trace of a smile appeared on Master Subhodi's face. Being a great sage, he already knew about Monkey and exactly what Monkey wanted to learn. But still he asked Monkey, "Tell me what you wish to learn."

I want to live forever, Monkey started to say, but he decided he should be modest. So he said instead, "I wish to learn any kind of wisdom you can teach me."

Master Subhodi laughed gently. *Here is a naughty one,* he thought to himself. *I shall test him first.* So he said, "Monkey, there are three hundred and sixty schools of wisdom. We start with quietism. It teaches you about diet and meditation."

Monkey frowned. "Will . . . will it teach me how to live forever?"

"Certainly not."

"Ah. Then . . . I don't think I desire that kind of wisdom."

"Very well," said Master Subhodi. "What about the sacred scriptures? You'll learn to read about the philosophy of the great Buddha."

"Will that teach me how to live forever?"

"No."

"Ah. Then I'm afraid reading would be too boring for me. I'm a monkey, after all. I can't sit still."

"I see," said Master Subhodi. "Then what about the wisdom of exercises? You will learn to balance your yin and yang and develop your breathing powers."

"And will *that* teach me how to live forever?" asked Monkey, holding his breath.

"Not at all."

"Master," said Monkey, "I'm not good at things that are difficult. Can't you teach me something quick and easy?"

Now Master Subhodi seemed to lose his patience. "You won't learn this!" he cried. "You won't learn that! How dare you call yourself a student!" He stood up and strode over to Monkey.

The students gasped.

Master Subhodi stared hard into Monkey's eyes. Suddenly, he lifted his right hand and struck Monkey on the head—slap! slap! slap!—three times. Then he folded his hands behind his back and walked away.

The students were shocked. Never before had they seen the master lose his temper.

"Master!" Monkey cried out, and he chased the sage to the door. Master Subhodi turned, gave Monkey a very strange look, and walked off into an inner room.

The students glared at Monkey.

"Go back to your mountain, Monkey!"

one of them shouted. "I don't think Master wants to teach you."

Monkey ignored the taunts. He was truly puzzled. Had the master been trying to tell him something? A secret message, perhaps? But what? Monkey touched his head where Master had struck him.

Suddenly, a broad grin appeared on Monkey's face.

He was quite certain he knew the answer.

6

MONKEY BECOMES
A STUDENT

It was three o'clock in the morning. Deep in the cave, Monkey got out of bed. Still wearing his pajamas, he tiptoed to the back of the cave where Master Subhodi slept. As Monkey expected, the back door to the master's chamber was only half shut.

Monkey crept in and stood by the master's bed.

Master Subhodi sat up instantly.

"You wretched monkey! What on earth are you doing here?"

"But you told me to come," Monkey said.

Master Subhodi frowned.

"Master," Monkey insisted, "when you hit me on the head three times, you were telling me to visit you at three o'clock in the morning. When you folded your hands behind your back, it was a sign I should come through the back door. So," finished Monkey with a grin, "here I am."

Master Subhodi gazed shrewdly at Monkey. *Ha,* he thought, *this monkey is truly the product of Heaven and Earth. He's the first one who has been able to read my secret signs. Perhaps he really can become an immortal.*

"All right, little monkey," Master Subhodi said, "I will accept you as a student. But you will need to study very hard."

Monkey did a somersault of delight.

Master Subhodi shook his head. "Monkey," he said, "is that the proper way to show your teacher respect?"

Hastily, Monkey made a deep, clumsy bow. He made sure his paw hid his grin of joy.

From that day on, Monkey became Master Subhodi's favorite student. He studied during the day with the other students and at night, secretly, with the master alone. Soon Monkey learned many things that the other students did not know.

He learned transformations that allowed him to turn himself into anything he wished. He developed vision that enabled him to see things thousands of miles away. He memorized whole books of magical spells that gave him undreamed-of powers, enabling him to stay young for centuries.

But after studying hard for one whole year, Monkey King began to get bored. One morning, Master Subhodi was giving a lecture. All the students were listening intently—all except Monkey. He kept pulling his ears, scratching his armpits, and poking the students sitting next to him.

Master Subhodi stopped his lecture. "Monkey? What are you doing?"

"Master, I—I was so excited by your lecture, I couldn't sit still," Monkey fibbed.

"Too excited to listen, hmm?" the master asked. "I hear that you have not been behaving well recently. Is that true?"

"No, I am a good student, Master! I study hour after hour. And when I am not studying, I'm working. I sweep the floors and hoe the community gardens—"

"That's not true, Master," said one of the other students. "Yesterday, while everybody else was hoeing, Monkey was in the peach tree eating all the fruit."

"And when he was supposed to be fetching water from the stream," said another student, "he sat in the river and took a bath."

"And when he was supposed to be sweeping," said yet another, "he made piles of dust, climbed a tree, and dumped the dust on our heads."

"Monkey," asked Master Subhodi, "are all these things true?"

"Master," Monkey replied, "there are reasons for everything. When I was in the peach tree, I was just testing the peaches, making sure you had only the best ones. The swimming in the stream . . . well, I was only trying to make my body as clean and pure as my mind. As for dropping dust . . ." Monkey paused, trying to think up a good excuse. "I . . . was working on my cloud soaring. That's why the dust flew up." Monkey showed them how he jumped, making sure

to kick up some dust.

"So, Monkey, it sounds as if you have been working hard on your cloud soaring. Please, be good enough to give us a demonstration."

Monkey was delighted to have the chance to show off. He put his feet together, breathed deeply, and jumped. Monkey soared high into the air, caught a little cloud, and rode it for a few seconds. Next moment, however, Monkey crashed to the ground in front of the master.

"Ha-ha-ha!" Master Subhodi burst out laughing. "Do you call that cloud soaring?" he asked. "At best, I think it should be called cloud crawling."

Monkey did not know what to say.

"A true cloud soarer," said the master, "can start at the Northern Sea, cross the Eastern, Western, and Southern Seas, and land again at the Northern Sea. One hundred and eight thousand leagues. That's real cloud soaring."

"A hundred and eight thousand leagues?" exclaimed Monkey, opening his eyes wide.

"Exactly! And you—who think you know everything—what about the Three Calamities?"

"Wh—what are they?"

"The Three Calamities are celestial wind, water, and fire. They are sent down by Jade Emperor every five hundred years. And if you don't know how to ward them off, you will perish."

"Perish!" cried Monkey. He was stunned.

7

MONKEY TRANSFORMS HIMSELF

When Monkey heard Master Subhodi say that the Three Calamities could cause his death, he exclaimed, "But, Master, I thought you taught me the secret of everlasting life—so I will never die."

"Monkey," sighed Master Subhodi. "All you have learned is how to stay young for a long time and a few magic tricks. Oh yes, and a few transformations. But you're not even close to knowing the secret of life."

Monkey jumped up and bowed his head to the ground. "Master," he cried, "have mercy on me. Teach me how to become a true immortal."

Master Subhodi studied Monkey's face. "Listen carefully," he said after a long pause. "There is no limit to knowledge. If you want to stay here as my student, you must first

40

obey the rules. If you don't, you will be dismissed. Do you understand?"

"Yes, I understand," Monkey said anxiously. "But, Master, do you think I can truly learn the secret of life? It sounds awfully difficult."

"Monkey, nothing in the world is too difficult. It's our thoughts that make it seem so. All you have to do is work hard."

"Master, from this moment forward I promise to be good. And I'll work and study as hard as possible," said Monkey. To show that he meant it, Monkey did a triple somersault.

True to his word, Monkey worked and studied diligently from that day on. He spent most of his time reciting spells, memorizing formulas, and listening to his master's lessons. Even in his dreams, Monkey shouted spells while kicking his legs and waving his arms.

Five years passed. Monkey became the master's most advanced student. Even Master Subhodi was beginning to think Monkey was well on his way to immortality.

All of this knowledge and power went to Monkey's head.

One summer afternoon, when all the students were practicing their lessons in front of the cave, Monkey started getting bored again. He strolled around, looking at what the other students were doing.

He stopped in front of one student. "Ha! Do you call that a transformation?" Monkey laughed. "Your lower body has changed into a crocodile, but look at your top. It looks like a donkey."

"It's easy to make fun, Monkey," said another student. "But what about you? What transformations can you do?"

"I can change myself into anything I want," boasted Monkey. "Do you want me to show you?"

"No, don't," another student cried. "Master Subhodi warned us never to use our spiritual powers without a good reason."

"But I have a good reason," Monkey said. "It's to show you that I am smarter than all of you. Now, watch this!"

Monkey leaped into a clear spot. Reciting

a magic formula, he shook himself. At once he vanished in a cloud of pink smoke. When the smoke cleared, there stood a beautiful peach tree with ripened peaches hanging from every branch.

"Bravo, Monkey!" the students cried, breaking into loud applause and laughter. "You are wonderful!"

Just then, Master Subhodi came out of the cave and walked through the crowd of students. He did not utter a single word. But as soon as the students saw him they grew quiet and sat down.

Monkey, however, had not noticed. Still a peach tree, he said proudly, "Of course I am wonderful. Sure, Master taught us the magic formulas. But if I weren't so smart, the formulas would have been useless. I'm the one who makes them work."

"I think," said Master Subhodi slowly, "that this peach tree knows almost everything . . . except the rules."

His voice was soft, but it sounded like thunder to Monkey. Quickly, Monkey transformed back into his true form and bowed low before the master.

"Master, please forgive me," he cried. "I didn't know you were here."

"Ah, my brilliant student. I see you have forgotten your promise to be good."

"We were just having a bit of fun, Master," pleaded Monkey.

"I won't punish you." The master sighed. "But you cannot stay here any longer."

Monkey burst into tears. "Master, I promise I'll never disobey you again."

"It's too late." Master Subhodi shook his head firmly. "Although you have learned much, you are far from the path of enlightenment. I cannot have students who just want to show off. It's too dangerous. And disrespectful."

"But—but what about those Three Calamities you talked about?" Monkey cried. "I haven't finished my studies. I am not an immortal yet."

"That is your own fault, Monkey," said the sage. "You must leave immediately. I advise you to use the powers you have learned for good causes. And I wish you

45

luck." Then Master Subhodi turned and walked away.

Monkey started to cry. All the same, he bowed deeply toward his master's back three times. Then he said goodbye to the other students and walked away from the cave.

As he sadly left his friends and his wise teacher behind, he wailed, "What will happen to me now?"

8

MONKEY MEETS A DEMON

Monkey slowly made his way across hills and streams and back out of the dark forest. At first he was sad, but when he remembered that he would soon be home with his monkey clan, his heart grew cheerful again. He had missed them terribly, and he could hardly wait to show them all the magic powers and tricks he had learned.

Monkey leaped up into the sky and lassoed a cloud. Within three blinks of an eye he was floating above the Mountain of Flowers and Fruits.

He jumped down from the cloud and somersaulted right in front of the waterfall. "Dear friends!" he cried. "I'm back!"

There was no answer.

Monkey looked around. Everything was in ruins. Even the trees were bare. "Dear monkeys," he shouted again, "your magnificent king has returned!"

Several monkeys peeked out cautiously from behind rocks and trees. "It is he!" they shouted. "Our king is back!" At once, thousands of cheering and jumping monkeys ran to Monkey. They hugged him and kissed him from the top of his head to the soles of his feet.

"Magnificent King," said one, "our eyes are worn out from looking for you every day. You have been gone so long." The monkeys began to weep.

"Why are you crying?" asked Monkey. "And why were you hiding when I arrived? What has happened here?"

"We have been attacked by a terrible demon who has captured many of our brothers and sisters."

"How dare he!" Monkey exploded. "Who is this demon? Where does he live?"

"He is called the Demon of Havoc. We don't know where he lives. He comes like a tornado and goes like a hurricane. He fills the sky with darkness and roaring."

"He sounds horrible," said Monkey, "but don't worry. I'll get him!" With that Monkey sprang high into the sky and searched, for thousands of leagues, with his penetrating vision.

Far to the north he spied a mountain covered with a swirling dark mist. "Ah ha!" cried Monkey. "I see where he lives."

Grabbing hold of a cloud, Monkey darted off to the misty mountain and then jumped down, landing right next to a vast hole in the ground. A dark, stinking wind was billowing out of the pit.

"Demon of Havoc!" Monkey shouted. "I am the Magnificent Monkey King! I've come to get my monkeys back!"

"Who is this king who dares to challenge me?" a furious voice screamed from the deep, dark hole. The next moment the demon himself leaped out.

He was enormous, with bulging cloud-shaped muscles all over his body. His mouth blew puffs of hot winds. His eyes were fireballs. He had a bristling beard made of icicles. In each of his huge hands he carried a bolt of lightning.

"Are *you* the king?" the demon cried, breaking into thunderous laughter. "You're not even three feet high. It's a shame I have to waste my energy killing someone as puny as you."

"You braggart!" Monkey roared. "Release my monkeys, Demon, or you'll regret it!"

The demon laughed. "I won't even need my swords to fight you!" he cried. And he threw his lightning bolts away.

The fight began. Though Monkey was small, his fists were like cannonballs. Soon the demon was panting from Monkey's heavy blows. Desperate, the demon snatched up his lightning-bolt swords.

At this, Monkey made himself invisible. "Here I am! Here I am!" he cried, leaping here, there, everywhere. The demon struck madly, but each time he struck nothing but air. Each blow was accompanied by a tremendous clap of thunder. Finally, the demon began to get tired.

Seeing his chance, Monkey plucked a

handful of golden hairs from his own leg and blew them into the air. "Alalalatola!" he shouted. At the word, every hair turned into hundreds of tiny monkeys. These tiny monkeys swarmed all over the demon— pulling, kicking, even tickling him. They knocked him down, and he couldn't get up again.

Meanwhile, Monkey appeared again in his natural form and leaped down into the demon's lair. It stank terribly, but Monkey ignored it. He plunged in deeper. In a far corner of the cave he found his monkey friends, hundreds of them, tied together like trapped crabs.

Monkey cut their cords. "Hurry!" he cried. "We're going home!"

The monkeys followed their king out of the hole. The Demon of Havoc was still lying on the ground, and sitting on the demon's chest were the hundreds of tiny monkeys.

"Alalalatola!" shouted Monkey, and instantly the tiny monkeys turned back into a handful of golden hair, which Monkey patted back onto his leg.

The demon was afraid to move. "Never hurt my clan again," Monkey warned, "or it will be even worse for you.

"Now, my friends," he said to the monkeys, "close your eyes."

He waved his hands and his tail in a magical pattern, conjuring up a great wind of his own. And in less than a wink, they were off.

"We're going home," Monkey cried as they flew through the air. "Once we get there, I have something very important to do."

9

MONKEY GOES TO THE SEA

As soon as they arrived home, the Monkey King called a meeting of all the monkeys.

"Dear friends," he said solemnly, "As your king, my most important duty is to protect you. From this experience with the Demon of Havoc, I have learned that we have to be strong so that no one can bully us again. I have a plan." Monkey leaped to his throne. "I will teach you all that I have learned from my teacher, Master Subhodi. Together we will build our Mountain of Flowers and Fruits into a mighty and powerful nation. No one will be able to defeat us. No one!"

Starting the next day, Monkey began to organize his kingdom. He appointed gibbon generals and baboon officers, and divided other monkeys into small units. Every day, Monkey watched while his generals and officers led the monkey teams in marching, drilling, and combat. He also taught them some of the magic tricks he had learned. He was satisfied to see them growing strong.

One morning, Monkey was demonstrating a difficult move with a tree branch. He waved his weapon vigorously, but the tree branch slipped out of his paw again and again. Frustrated, Monkey threw the tree branch to the ground. "As your king, my most important duty is to protect you. But I don't even have a decent weapon. In my fight with the Demon of Havoc, all I had were my fists and my brains. I was lucky to win. What I really need now is a good weapon. Not just any weapon, however. Since I am special, it must be special, too."

Grandmother Monkey stood up. "Your Majesty, you should not use an ordinary weapon, of course. Well, my grandfather told me that he learned, from his grandfather, that at the bottom of the Eastern Sea there lives a dragon king who has many

55

special weapons. But the trouble is, he lives underwater."

"Underwater!" cried Monkey. "Tcha! A small matter. I can't be harmed by water, fire, or wind. Of course I can visit this dragon king."

So saying, he ran to the iron bridge, recited a spell, and jumped into the churning water below. At once, a whirlpool caught him and carried him straight down to the bottom of the Eastern Sea in front of the Dragon Palace.

How beautiful it was! The palace was made entirely of white coral and was studded with thousands of gleaming pearls. Thousands of crabs mounted on the backs of sea horses stood guard, commanded by bright-red lobster generals. But Dragon King himself was the most magnificent sight. Majestic and dignified, he surveyed his kingdom from his throne, which was made from the back of a gigantic sea turtle.

Dragon King looked surprised—and a little nervous, too—to see Monkey. Only a greatly powerful being could appear at the bottom of the sea. "Welcome, sir," he said politely. "What can I do for you?"

"It's embarrassing to ask you a favor on my first visit." Monkey grinned. "But I am the Magnificent Monkey King, and I need a suitable weapon for myself, the better to defend my clan. I was told you had many magical weapons to spare."

What a rude request! thought Dragon King. He did not like Monkey, but he dared not refuse. "I don't have many weapons to spare," he said. "But for you . . . let me see what I can do." Dragon King stood up and clapped his hands. "Let the hammerhead shark come forth!" he called out loudly.

The hammerhead shark swam forward and offered Monkey a huge hammer.

Monkey King barely glanced at it. "A hammer is too ordinary a weapon for me," he said. "Surely you can do better."

Twin spirals of smoke bubbled out of Dragon King's nose. But he only said, "Let the swordfish enter!"

The swordfish swam into view and offered an enormous sword.

Monkey tried a few thrusts. "Too light," he said, throwing the sword on the floor.

Dragon King turned blue with anger. But instead of exploding, he ordered again, "Let the narwhale enter."

A narwhale arrived and offered a gigantic pointy head spike.

"No, no. That's much too ugly." Monkey waved it away. "It's not even worth touching."

Dragon King was nearly spitting fire. He glowered at Monkey. "I have nothing else to show you."

"Now, now," soothed Monkey. "That's not really true, is it?" He was suddenly attracted by a golden light coming from a room behind Dragon King's throne. "What is that?"

Without waiting for an answer, he barged into the room. It was Dragon King's treasure hall. But Monkey paid no attention to the gold and silver and jewels around him. His eyes were immediately drawn to a thick iron pillar in the center of the room. It was about a hundred feet long, and it glowed with beams of golden light.

"That," said Dragon King, who followed Monkey into the treasure hall, "is the magic pillar that holds the Sacred Island up on the sea surface. It weighs thirteen thousand five hundred pounds."

"Ah," said Monkey. "Is that so? It would be the perfect weapon for me, except it's too long and too thick."

Instantly, the pillar became much shorter and thinner. Everyone gasped, including Dragon King himself.

"It's magic!" Monkey cried. "How wonderful. A little shorter and thinner," he commanded the pillar. It shrank and shrank and shrank until it was the size of a toothpick.

"Now, larger . . . a little larger . . . ah!" When it was big enough to fit comfortably in his paw, Monkey grabbed it and examined it closely. Made of coal-black iron, it had golden clasps at both ends. It bore the inscription MAGIC STAFF WITH GOLDEN CLASPS.

Monkey tested it with a few thrusts and passes. Golden beams shot throughout the treasure hall.

"Splendid, splendid! Thanks, Dragon King!" Monkey turned to leave.

"But the Sacred Island!" Dragon King shouted. "It's going to float away!"

"I hope it has a good voyage," laughed Monkey as he ran out.

"Stop that thief!" cried Dragon King.

Instantly, forty-two thousand angry crabs, each with its pincers raised, swarmed forward. Monkey was surrounded by nipping, snapping claws!

They were closing in. Monkey stuck out his new weapon and began to spin. Faster and faster he turned, making a great funnel of water that the crabs could not penetrate.

"I'll pay you later," Monkey shouted. "Thanks!" He ran up the wall of the funnel, straight up to the surface of the water, and back to the iron bridge.

Monkey waved his shining new treasure over his head and exclaimed, "Now I am prepared for anything!"

10

MONKEY VISITS HEAVEN

It was early in the morning, and Jade Emperor, ruler of Heaven and Earth, had just put a cup of jasmine tea to his lips when Dragon King, crimson with anger, rushed into the throne room.

Dragon King bowed hurriedly, then burst out, "Your Majesty, I, your humble subject, beg you to bring the abominable monkey to justice. Otherwise, peace is impossible."

Then he told Jade Emperor how Monkey had stolen the magic pillar. "Now the Sacred Island is bobbing around the sea like a lost rowboat. It is a calamity!

"This monkey is too much for me," Dragon King continued. "Our only hope is that you, Ruler of Heaven and Earth, will send soldiers to capture this pest and restore the peace."

"Outrageous!" exclaimed Jade Emperor, sneezing three times. Jade Emperor always sneezed when he was upset. "Who is this dreadful monkey?" he asked his ministers.

Thousand-League Eye stepped forward. "Your Majesty, do you remember that strange light you once saw a long time ago? I told you then it was a little monkey. He is the one of whom Dragon King speaks."

"He didn't have much power then," added Thousand-League Ear. "But over the years it seems he has learned many things."

"I see," said Jade Emperor, and he stroked his long white beard. "Dragon King, return to the bottom of the Eastern Sea. Be assured, I shall take care of this matter."

Dragon King bowed and went back home.

"It would be easy enough to defeat this monkey," Jade Emperor mused out loud. "But since he was born of Heaven and Earth, I will invite him to Heaven so we can keep an eye on him. If he behaves well, we can promote him. If he misbehaves, we can arrest him at any time." Jade Emperor nodded at his own wisdom.

"Splendid idea." "Brilliant strategy," Jade Emperor's ministers exclaimed.

"Go fetch him!" Jade Emperor said to Thousand-League Eye. "But wait! Whatever you do, don't tell him my plan. Just say I am inviting him to . . . visit Heaven."

Thousand-League Eye sped off and came before Monkey in his palace on the mountain. Monkey was delighted by the invitation. "A visit to Heaven! Well, it's about time someone realized how important I am."

With that he somersaulted upon a cloud and soared off toward the North Star. In his rush to get to Heaven, Monkey completely forgot that not everyone, even Immortals, could leap as far as a hundred and eight thousand leagues. In an instant, he was already at the southern gate of Heaven. Thousand-League Eye was left far behind.

Monkey walked toward the southern gate proudly. But two guards blocked his way.

"Where do you think you're going?" they asked him.

"I was invited by Jade Emperor," Monkey said in a loud voice, expecting to see a big reaction.

The guards didn't answer. Instead, they lifted their swords and spears.

"Didn't you hear me? I am the guest of Jade Emperor," Monkey sputtered, pushing the guards to the side. But they pushed him back, firmly.

"How dare you! Do you know who I am? I am the Magnificent Monkey King of the Mountain of Flowers and Fruits, and I wouldn't have come here if I hadn't been invited." Monkey was puffing out the anger now. He took the magic staff from behind his ear and was about to enlarge it to have a real fight, when Thousand-League Eye finally arrived behind him, out of breath.

Seeing him, Monkey shouted, "You old fraud! You told me I was invited by Jade Emperor, so why are these cutthroats holding me up?"

"Well, you have never been here before and no one knows you. Of course the guards won't let you in." Thousand-League Eye panted. "You could have saved a lot of trouble if you had just waited for me." He rolled his eyes, admonishing Monkey.

Swallowing his anger, Monkey followed Thousand-League Eye.

When they entered the southern gate of Heaven, Monkey's mouth opened with awe. Seventy-two magnificent temples and thirty-three glorious palaces stood before him. He saw dazzling bridges adorned with jade in the shape of phoenixes and huge pillars carved with golden dragons. He saw flowers and animals he had never seen on Earth. Golden bells rang and tower drums beat, while a troupe of magical spirits danced.

Monkey clapped his hands in delight. "Heaven is indeed heaven!" he cried.

Monkey changed into suitable court clothing and was then introduced to the Emperor himself.

"So," said Jade Emperor slowly, "you are that monkey I've heard so much about. How do you like Heaven so far?"

"Oh, it's marvelous," Monkey said sincerely.

"Would you like to live here, then?" Jade Emperor asked. He smiled secretly to himself.

"Live here?" said Monkey. "Me? For how long?"

"As long as you work for me."

"Work?" Monkey was surprised. He grabbed Thousand-League Eye's sleeve. "You told me this was just a visit."

Turning back to Jade Emperor, Monkey exclaimed, "I am Magnificent Monkey King. Why should I work for you? I'm going home." Monkey turned around and was about to scamper off.

"Wait!" shouted Jade Emperor. He was surprised by Monkey's quick temper. "What if I put you . . . put you in charge of something important?"

"Important?" Monkey stopped. "Like what?" he turned back, demanding.

"Em . . ." Jade Emperor searched his brain. "How would you like to be the Heavenly Horse Deity?"

"Is it an important position?" Monkey studied Jade Emperor's face.

"Oh, definitely." Jade Emperor nodded solemnly. "It involves transportation in all of Heaven. Very important."

"Hmm," Monkey contemplated. "I have been a king on Earth, but never in charge of anything in Heaven. It might be fun to be important in Heaven for a while."

Thinking of this, Monkey quickly made a deep bow and cried, "Sure, I'll do it." Though he had no idea what the job would entail, he was grinning from ear to ear. He was already imagining himself as a well-respected heavenly official. He thought about his monkey friends back on the Mountain of Flowers and Fruits, and he wished they could see him now!

11

MONKEY AS A HEAVENLY HORSE DEITY

Escorted by his assistants, Monkey was led to an enormous structure. At first glance, Monkey was not very impressed. It looked just like a big round arena with a high ceiling. But once Monkey stepped inside, he gasped at the lovely sight that greeted him. Inside was a garden filled with flowers, trees, and small streams winding throughout. The ceiling was made of misted glass, so the garden was full of soft morning sunlight. And the horses! Roaming about the garden freely here and there were hundreds of horses, the likes of which Monkey had never seen on Earth. They were all white, almost transparent; their beautiful wings and fluffy tails danced gracefully as they flew around inside the arena, their bridles and saddles shining with jewels and golden embroidery.

Monkey fell instantly in love with this place. Heavenly horses! No wonder Jade Emperor said that this was an important job! Hastily, he climbed up onto one tall and handsome horse. Oh, this was not riding! It was floating. Monkey melted with joy. This was indeed heavenly and celestial!

When Monkey finally got off the horse, he knew that he would be very happy in this job.

Early the next morning, after he washed himself carefully and dressed up in his court robe, Monkey walked to the Heavenly Stable surrounded by his assistants. Holding his paws behind his back, Monkey walked around the building and started giving orders to everyone.

He came up behind the cooks who were busy preparing the magical horse food. He tapped one on the back, saying, "Hurry up, the horses are hungry."

Then, he craned his head over the shoulders of the grooms who were cleaning and brushing the horses. "Look," pointed

Monkey, "you've missed a spot of dirt behind his ear!"

After that, he watched the horse trainer who was conducting exercises with the horses. "Oh no, no, no!" Monkey exclaimed loudly, "You must first balance yourself with the yin and yang before the exercises. Otherwise the spirit will never pass through the horses."

Monkey was enjoying himself immensely. He felt that he was made for this job of bossing and giving advice. Still, a monkey's span of attention is not very long. Soon he became bored and decided to take a walk outside.

As he wandered around Heaven, he warmly introduced himself to all the important people he met along the way. "I am the new Heavenly Horse Deity," he told them proudly. "I'm in charge of transportation in all of Heaven." Then he invited some of these officials back to the Heavenly Stable and had a wonderful flying-horse ride with them. Afterward, they went to sit down in his office, laughing, chatting, joking, and eating. Monkey put his feet up on his desk and told his new friends all about his life on the Mountain of Flowers and Fruits. He was having a terrific time as the boss of Heavenly Stable.

A week soon passed by, and Monkey did the same thing every day—a few minutes of supervising in the morning, and the rest of the day was spent lounging around with his new friends.

One day, Monkey was eating lunch with several other officials.

"How do you like your new job?" the official in charge of the heavenly plants asked.

"Great," Monkey swallowed a mouthful of food, and replied. "As you can see, the horses are healthy and happy. The horse riding is marvelous. And, on the top of that, I like to be in a position of such importance."

The officials looked at each other slyly, snickering secretly behind their hands. "Hey, I want to ask you something." Monkey stopped eating, hiccuped, then asked confidently, "What is the exact rank of my position? I have been wondering about it. Can you please tell me?"

The officials looked at each other and said nothing.

"Come on, tell me. Don't be shy." Monkey joked.

The officials shook their heads.

"Don't play games with me. What is my rank?" Monkey demanded.

"Well, there is . . . there is no ranking for your position." The official in charge of heavenly dew said.

"No ranking? Oh, because my position is too high?" Monkey said, and smiled excitedly.

"No, no, no," the Heavenly Dew Deity burst into a chuckle, but stopped himself at once. "Never mind. Never mind." He ate a big bite of food and tried to change the subject.

"No, you have to tell me!" Monkey was stern now.

"Well, the truth is, your position is too low to be ranked," the Heavenly Dew Deity said boldly. "You see, your job doesn't even have a salary. If you do well, the most you will get is some praise, and a pat on the back.

But if something bad happens," he added, "YOU are the one to be punished. . . ."

"It's impossible!" Monkey cried. "Didn't Jade Emperor say this was an important position?" Monkey turned red all over.

"You can ask them if you don't believe me." The Heavenly Dew Deity pointed to other officials around the table.

They all nodded in agreement.

"Outrageous!" Monkey roared, pounding the cup on the table. "Who does Jade Emperor think I am? A hired hand? A stable groom? I am a king, just like him. Forget this job. I am leaving." As he made this announcement, he tore off the court robe and threw it to the ground.

The officials were shocked. They didn't expect such a strong reaction from Monkey at all. Now they were frightened, for none of them wanted to be held responsible for Monkey's leaving. They picked up the court robe and rushed after him, dragging and pulling, and begging him to stay. Monkey, however, pushed and shoved the officials away while striding toward the southern gate of Heaven.

Jade Emperor and his ministers were in the middle of a ceremony near the Milky Way Fountain when they heard a ruckus and saw Monkey coming toward them, surrounded by the pleading officials.

"What is it? Why so loud?" Jade Emperor frowned. "Bring them here."

Monkey and the officials stopped in front of Jade Emperor.

"Monkey . . . I mean Heavenly Horse Deity, why are you here instead of working at the stable?" Jade Emperor asked.

"Don't try to fool me." Monkey exploded. "You told me this was an important position, but actually it doesn't even have a rank. I am leaving."

"How dare you speak to His Majesty like this?!" Jade Emperor's ministers were outraged. "For your rudeness you deserve a thousand deaths!"

"Wait a minute," Jade Emperor waved at them to calm them down. Then he turned to Monkey. "So what is this? You don't like the job?"

"Who said I don't like the job?" Monkey retorted. "I like the job, but I don't like the ranking. I am Magnificent Monkey King. You know, a king?" Monkey straightened his head and glared at Jade Emperor.

"You are small, but your temper is quite large," Jade Emperor said sarcastically. "What if I offer you a truly important job now?"

"I don't care. I am going home." Monkey turned around and was about to walk away.

Jade Emperor thought quickly. He knew a thing or two about Monkey by now and, in an instant, he had come up with an idea.

"Monkey, stop!" he called out. "I think I have the perfect position for you! How about being in charge of the Heavenly Peach Garden?"

Monkey stopped dead in his tracks. *Peach garden?* he thought. *How did Jade Emperor know that peaches are my favorite food?* He turned around.

"Do you mean to say that I'll be the boss of the whole peach garden, with no one above me?"

"No one but me, of course."

"Does this job have a rank?"

"Absolutely," Jade Emperor smiled.

Well, since I am here already, I might as well give it a try. I can leave anytime if I don't like it, Monkey thought to himself.

"I accept," Monkey exclaimed, smiling. "I love peaches. Heavenly peaches should be delicious."

"No, no," warned Jade Emperor. "Your job is to protect the peaches, not eat them. Is that clearly understood?"

"Er, yes," said Monkey. He knew that he would have the final say as soon as he got there.

12

MONKEY IN THE HEAVENLY
PEACH GARDEN

Early the next morning a very excited Monkey was escorted by several officials to the Heavenly Peach Garden. Soon he would be surrounded by peaches! He had hardly slept at the thought.

When he passed through the high garden gates and saw what lay beyond, Monkey's eyes bulged out. A long path lined with rubies circled in and around the peach trees, leading to eight red pagodas carved with golden dragons. Four dazzling water fountains made the entire garden glisten with a million misty rainbows.

But the most astonishing sight was the peach trees. There were not one, not two, but *three* different kinds! Some had pink leaves and some had gold, while others had purple leaves with silver veins. And the peaches! They were as big as melons, ivory-white, and almost transparent.

Monkey fairly swooned with delight. "How . . . how many trees are here?" he asked a gardener.

"Three thousand six hundred," the gardener said proudly. "The first two thousand—the ones with pink leaves—bear peaches that ripen every three thousand years. Whoever eats them becomes joyful and wise. The peaches on the next thousand trees—the ones with golden leaves—ripen once every six thousand years. Whoever eats them will stay young forever."

"Six thousand years! My goodness!" Monkey was impressed. "But what about these, the ones with purple leaves and silver veins?"

"Those six hundred are the most precious trees of all," the gardener whispered. "Their peaches ripen once in nine thousand years. Whoever eats them will live forever."

Monkey could hardly contain himself. Live forever! He stared at one of the peaches. It was almost calling him to smell it, touch it . . . taste it. But Monkey restrained himself. He was in charge of the garden, after all.

Sighing, he followed behind the gardeners, who had gone off to make an inventory of all the trees and their fruit. But Monkey could not concentrate. His mouth was watering. His stomach was growling. The air was ripe with the tempting aroma of peaches.

"This is silly," he finally said to himself. "I am the boss of this garden! After all, how will I know the difference between a good peach and a bad peach unless I try one? Only one, of course. No one will even miss it."

He called the gardeners. "Attention! Here is my first order as head of this garden. I am very tired." He let out a huge yawn. "I need to take a nap in that pagoda, but I need perfect quiet. Wait outside the garden. As soon as I wake up, I'll call you and you can continue working."

The gardeners bowed and left. As soon as they were gone, Monkey closed the gate and ran to the purple-leaved trees, where he searched for the largest, ripest, best peach of them all. And at last he found it. He jumped onto the branch and sat next to the peach.

My, it was beautiful! Monkey leaned down to smell it better. What sweetness it promised! His stomach would not stop growling. Carefully, Monkey plucked the peach from its stem and cupped it in his paws. It was almost too beautiful to eat . . . but that would not stop him.

Monkey took a tiny bite . . . and almost fainted. The peach was cool, sweet, and juicy—the most delicious thing he'd ever tasted. He took another bite. And another . . . and in no time at all Monkey had gobbled up the entire peach! And no sooner had he eaten one than he *had* to have another!

"Surely just *one* more peach won't make a difference," he told himself. "There are so many." So Monkey ate a second peach, and then a third . . . and then more and more, until his belly was almost bursting, it was so full.

Then he went back to the gates and called the gardeners back in. "Time to work," he said severely.

Every day from then on, while he pretended to take a nap, Monkey ate as many peaches as possible from the purple-leafed trees. "Let others become immortal by studying," he said with a laugh. "I will become immortal by eating!"

One afternoon, Monkey was eating his peaches as usual when he heard the gates open. Someone was coming into the garden! Alarmed, he transformed himself into a tiny caterpillar, hid under a leaf, and waited.

Presently seven fairies entered, carrying baskets. They were collecting peaches for the Jade Emperor's Peach Banquet. The fairies gathered three baskets of peaches from the pink-leafed trees and another three baskets of peaches from the golden-leafed trees. But when they came to the purple-leafed trees, they found no ripe peaches at all. Not one!

"Where have all the ripe peaches gone?" they asked one another.

Monkey kept very, very still.

"It seems to me," one of the fairies said, "that someone has been stealing Jade Emperor's peaches. The Emperor must be informed at once!"

And the fairies turned around and began to run toward the gates.

13

MONKEY GOES
TO A BANQUET

The fairies were going to report the missing peaches! Monkey thought quickly. In a blink he transformed back to himself and jumped down from the tree. "Thieves! Thieves!" he yelled at the seven fairies. "How dare you steal my peaches!"

The fairies fell trembling to their knees. "Master, we are not thieves!" they protested. "We were sent by Jade Emperor to fetch peaches for the Peach Banquet!"

"Ah," said Monkey, becoming instantly friendly. "So you serve Jade Emperor?"

"Yes, Master."

"Well, well. Get up and tell me about this Peach Banquet. What is it?"

"It's the biggest banquet ever given by Jade Emperor. It is held once every thousand years at Jade Pond," one of the fairies replied timidly.

"Who will be there?" Monkey asked.

"Great Buddha, for one. Goddess Guan-yin, for another. And many others, such as the Emperors of the Four Quarters, the Five Spirits of the Pole Star. . . . All the important high beings will be there."

"*All* the important beings?" Monkey snapped. "Then why haven't I been invited? I am the Magnificent Monkey King, head of the Heavenly Peach Garden, am I not? How dare Jade Emperor not invite *me?*"

"We—we don't know," said the fairies, beginning to tremble before Monkey's anger.

"Well," said Monkey, "since he didn't invite me, I'll have to invite myself. Magnificent Monkey King intends to enjoy all the pleasures of Heaven." He straightened his court hat and robes and groomed his fur. But then, out of the corner of his eye, he saw the seven fairies edging away.

"Wait. Where do you think you're going?" Monkey lifted a paw, recited a magic formula, and shouted, "Stay!" His freezing spell instantly froze the fairies in mid-motion. With a satisfied grin on his face, Monkey somersaulted out of the

Heavenly Peach Garden and headed for Jade Pond.

On the way, Monkey saw in front of him a goddess in elegant court clothing riding a cloud. *She must be going to the banquet, too,* he thought. A great surge of jealousy came over him. He blinked his eyes a few times and figured out a quick plan. Monkey ran after the goddess.

"Respectable goddess, where are you going?" he called.

"To Jade Pond," the goddess replied. "I, Lotus-Feet Immortal, have been invited to Jade Emperor's Peach Banquet," she said proudly.

Monkey feigned surprise. "Oh, haven't you heard the news? Jade Emperor has asked all the guests to go to Cloud Palace instead of Jade Pond this time. It's a little farther away, but it's more spacious."

"Really?" said the goddess. "Then I had better hurry, or I will be late." She turned her cloud around and flew off in the opposite direction.

"Clever monkey!" Monkey congratulated himself. "Now you *are* invited!" He recited a spell, transforming himself into an identical copy of Lotus-Feet Immortal. Then he headed for Jade Pond.

When Monkey reached Jade Pond, he was surprised to find it quiet. No guests had arrived yet. Servants were running back and forth carrying dishes and refreshments and going over the last details for the great banquet.

Monkey was wondering what to do when he smelled something marvelous. It was a fragrance sweeter than honey and delicate as the scent of the rare green rose. Monkey followed the scent into the kitchen. And there, bubbling over a small flame, was an immense silver pot. It bore a label:

LAUGHING LIQUID

Sure enough, the bubbling liquid made a sound like laughter. Monkey closed his eyes and breathed in the aroma. It tickled his nose, and he giggled. *Oh,* he thought, *for one tiny taste . . .*

Monkey checked the door. No one was watching. He reached into the pot, put the tip of his little finger into the liquid, and then licked it. Delicious! Monkey giggled. He wanted another taste. He put his paw in the liquid and scooped out a mouthful. Aaah . . . a delectable current flowed down his tongue, his throat, and his stomach—until it seemed to reach everywhere inside his body. Monkey chuckled. But he wanted still more! He put his whole head into the pot and drank and drank and drank. Within moments, all the liquid was gone.

Feeling a little dizzy, Monkey sat on the floor. A strange sensation swept over him. And then he began to laugh. He tried to stop, but he couldn't. The laughs started with chortles, giggles, snickers, and chuckles, but then they became bigger. Soon Monkey was guffawing, belly laughing, slapping his legs, howling—whatever kind of laugh there was, Monkey was laughing them all and could not stop.

In the midst of Monkey's laughter a great gong sounded. Then the booming voice of Jade Emperor could be heard: "Let the Peach Banquet begin!"

14

MONKEY AT THE PEACH BANQUET

At the sound of Jade Emperor's voice, Monkey climbed to his feet. Although he was still laughing uncontrollably, he knew he was in deep trouble. *I had better slip away,* he thought. He staggered to the doorway to make his escape.

But it was too late. The guests had arrived. Jade Emperor was seated at the head of the great banquet table. All around him were dozens of high gods and immortals. As Monkey hesitated in the doorway, Jade Emperor looked up. "Ah! Lotus-Feet Immortal, where have you been?"

Monkey suddenly remembered that he was still disguised as the old goddess. He opened his mouth to say something polite. But instead of words, great gales of laughter burst out. All the gods and goddesses at the table turned and stared at him.

"Has something funny happened?" Jade Emperor asked with a frown. "Well, whatever it is, Lotus-Feet Immortal, come join us. But please do not laugh. We are discussing a very serious matter."

Biting his lips to keep from laughing, Monkey made his way to the table. To his amusement, he was seated right across the table from Dragon King of the Eastern Sea!

"Now, to answer your question, Dragon King," said Jade Emperor, "I have put Monkey in charge of the Heavenly Peach Garden. But my real plan is—"

Monkey King could not restrain himself. He broke out into another flood of giggles.

Jade Emperor looked gravely at Monkey. "Lotus-Feet Immortal, what do you find so funny?"

"Noth—noth—nothing," Monkey sputtered, and before he burst out again, he slapped his paws over his mouth. He grew redder and redder, until he felt he was about to explode with laughter.

"Very well," Jade Emperor said severely.

"But do try to control yourself. Now, as I was saying," he continued, "I have Monkey King working in the Peach Garden. It's a kind of an arrest, although he doesn't know that—"

Arrest! Monkey was furious! But all he could do was throw his head back and laugh more uproariously than ever. He laughed so wildly that he lost control of his transformation, just for a split second.

Across from Monkey, Dragon King of the Eastern Sea blinked. Then he jumped up, scurried around Monkey's chair, and screamed, "Ah ha! A monkey's tail. Look, Your Majesty! This is not Lotus-Feet Immortal! It's Monkey—in disguise!"

Monkey looked over his shoulder. Sure enough, his tail was showing. *Run away!* he thought to himself. *Go home!* He jumped to his feet. And before the gods and goddesses could do anything, Monkey was racing through the southern gate of Heaven. He dove into the sky and somersaulted down to Earth.

Meanwhile, at Jade Pond, there was a

great commotion. No sooner had Monkey escaped than the seven fairies who had been frozen in the Heavenly Peach Garden came running in. Monkey's spell had worn off.

"Great Jade Emperor," the fairies cried, "forgive us. That monkey has eaten hundreds of your peaches!"

They had hardly finished speaking when the real Lotus-Feet Immortal zoomed in on her cloud. "Your Majesty, forgive me for being so late, but a monkey I met told me that the banquet was at Cloud Palace."

Then a servant from the kitchen rushed in, panic-stricken. "Your Majesty! The Laughing Liquid is—is gone!" she cried.

Jade Emperor was furious! "Such chaos is totally unacceptable on such an important day. Thousand-League Eye, Thousand-League Ear, search out Monkey and see where he has gone. I am going to punish him severely!" Jade Emperor began sneezing repeatedly.

Both ministers rushed off. In a split second they were back.

"Monkey . . . is already back at the

Mountain of Flowers and Fruits," gasped Thousand-League Eye.

"And . . . he is still . . . laughing," huffed Thousand-League Ear.

Jade Emperor was enraged. He turned to his bravest general. "Vaisravane," he shouted, "I order you to take one hundred thousand soldiers and arrest this—this rascal . . . this rogue . . . this rapscallion . . . this wretched no-good monkey! Bring him to me immediately. He shall regret the day he ever set foot in Heaven!"

15

MONKEY UNDER ATTACK

Led by Vaisravane, one hundred thousand heavenly soldiers arrived at the Mountain of Flowers and Fruits and surrounded the Cave of the Water Curtain. They carried thousands of yellow battle flags upon which was written:

JADE EMPEROR BRINGS PEACE!

But Monkey was ready for them. Ten thousand monkeys were fanned out in front of his palace under a red and golden flag upon which was written:

MAGNIFICENT MONKEY KING,
EQUAL OF HEAVEN!

A trumpet sounded. Monkey appeared, dressed for battle. He wore a golden vest, a yellow cap with a golden band, and a pair of cloud-stepping boots. With his magic staff in his paw, he felt confident and powerful.

The two armies stood facing each other across a small stream. Battle drums began to beat, shaking every rock and tree on the mountain. Flags snapped in the wind like firecrackers.

General Natha, the son of General Vaisravane, buckled on his armor and stepped forward. In each of his hands he held a small wheel.

Monkey moved to meet him. Casually spinning his magic staff in his fingers, he smiled. "Hello, little brother. Are you out of your diapers yet? I don't have the heart to kill a baby."

"Shameless monkey!" Natha screamed. "Your crimes and insults deserve a thousand deaths. Here, taste my rings of fire!" As he spoke, the wheels in his hands burst into red-hot flames. Natha swung his arms around and around, flinging hundreds of fire wheels toward Monkey, who found himself in the middle of a swirling fireball.

Quickly Monkey pulled a hair from the

top of his head. "Alalalatola!" he cried. The hair turned into a huge hollow straw. Monkey stuck it into the stream and with one mighty breath—*whooosh!*—sucked up all the water. Then—*splooosh!*—Monkey blew the water out, drowning the flames instantly.

"This is fun!" Monkey laughed. "What else can you do?"

Vaisravane had lost the first battle. Now he called upon the Kings of the Four Quarters—North, South, East, and West. They were armed with sword, hook, axe, and spear.

"How dare you call yourself 'Equal of Heaven'!" they cried. "Wretched monkey, prepare to die!" They rushed upon Monkey.

"Hurrah!" cried Monkey, shaking his magic staff. Now a true battle began. Fighting all the kings at once, Monkey danced at the center of the circle. He leaped and jumped and swung his magic staff so quickly, it dazzled the kings' eyes. Weapons clanged. Blows rained down like thunder. Sparks flew through the air like falling stars.

Fifty blows—no winner. A hundred

blows—still no winner. The King of the North was so frustrated, he jumped into the air and blew himself away. The King of the South was so angry, he broke his sword in two and crawled away. The King of the West became so upset, he turned himself inside out and disappeared.

Only the King of the East fought on. Throwing away his spear, he pulled a small black bag out of his sleeve and threw it at Monkey's feet. The bag ballooned until it became as big as a whale and tried to swallow Monkey whole.

But Monkey was too quick. He wielded his magic staff and poked holes in the bag. Torn to shreds, the black bag blew away in the wind. The King of the East fled in panic.

"Hurrah for Magnificent Monkey King!" the monkey army cheered.

General Vaisravane was desperate. The battle had begun at dawn. Now it was twilight, and he had still not managed to catch Monkey. He ordered his heavenly army of one hundred thousand to attack. The soldiers, covered in armor from head to toe,

wielding swords and spears, rushed forward.

Monkey showed no concern. "I am the Magnificent Monkey King!" he declared. "Go back and tell Jade Emperor not to bother me anymore. Otherwise, I will come to his palace and tickle him until he topples from his dragon throne!" He plucked some golden hairs from his chest and threw them into the air.

"Alalalatola!" Instantly, each hair became ten thousand vicious wasps. The wasps swarmed over Jade Emperor's soldiers, stinging their faces and hands. The wasps crept under the soldiers' helmets and armor and into their boots, biting their ears, armpits, and toes. They were everywhere! One hundred thousand heavenly soldiers screamed, flung down their weapons, and fled.

Greatly ashamed, General Vaisravane returned to Jade Emperor and reported his defeat.

"Impossible!" cried Jade Emperor. "One hundred thousand heavenly soldiers could not catch one little monkey? Now what am I to do?" He let out a series of explosive sneezes that rocked the whole palace.

One of the Emperor's guests at the Peach Banquet, the Goddess Guan-yin, pressed her palms together. "Jade Emperor, I have an idea," she said. Leaning forward, she whispered into the Emperor's ear. "Send Magician Lang to catch him."

"Ah. Mmm. Yes." And Jade Emperor smiled.

16

MONKEY MEETS
MAGICIAN LANG

Magician Lang was called upon only for the most desperate of heavenly emergencies, although you would not know it to look at her. She was a very pretty, delicate-looking woman, with a pale face, finely arched eyebrows, and a small red mouth. She tied back her shining black hair, which reached her heels, with a yellow silk scarf, and wore a long gown as white as duck down. But in spite of her delicate appearance, she was the most cunning and skillful magician known in Heaven or on Earth.

When she arrived at the Mountain of Flowers and Fruits, Monkey's scouts rushed back to report the news.

Monkey strolled out to meet her. "Ah. A lovely woman." He bowed. "You would be better off finding a husband, really. You can't win against *me*."

Magician Lang's smooth pale face showed no emotion. "You are so sure of yourself," she said, "but I'll bet that I can defeat you in five rounds."

"Five rounds?" Monkey laughed and snapped his fingers. "I accept!"

At the sound of the snap, Magician Lang turned herself into a giant—fifty thousand feet tall, with scarlet hair, a blue face, and enormous teeth. In her massive hands she held a club as big as a tree. And she ran at Monkey, screaming, about to bring the club straight down upon his head!

At the last moment Monkey jumped aside. "Well, well, she's playing the transformation game." Monkey chuckled to himself. "She doesn't know that's my specialty!"

Instantly, he changed himself into a gray sparrow and darted into the leaves of a tall pine.

Magician Lang swiftly turned herself into a hawk and flew after him.

The sparrow wove in and out of the trees with blinding speed, flying high and low.

The hawk sped after in close pursuit. Suddenly the sparrow veered and dove into a dense thicket. The hawk put on an extra burst of speed to barrel through, but she got tangled in the thick underbrush.

"Round number one!" the sparrow declared. He flew down toward the ocean and changed himself into a fish.

The hawk turned herself into a shark and followed.

Deeper and deeper the fish swam, the shark right behind him. As the shark began to catch up, the fish saw a squid just ahead. He swam right between the tentacles. Following madly, the shark crashed into the squid, who was so angry he squirted black ink right into the shark's face.

"Round number two," the fish shouted cheerfully as he swam toward the shore. Leaping onto land, he changed himself into a green snake and slithered into the forest among the sticks and leaves.

Meanwhile, the shark washed off the squid ink, reached land, and turned herself into a gray crane, with a long sharp black beak shaped like a hook.

The snake zigzagged under the leaves; the gray crane swooped behind him. She had nearly nipped his tail with her black beak when the snake darted into a tiny hole in the ground.

"Round number three." The snake giggled and disappeared.

The gray crane had lost her target and was about to lose her temper. She took a deep breath and changed back into her original form. Looking around for Monkey, she spied an ancient temple on a nearby hilltop. It had one door, two windows, and a Buddha statue in the middle. Could Monkey be hiding in there?

Magician Lang was about to enter the temple when she came to a halt. She studied the building closely for a moment. Then she sat down, crossed her legs, and waited. After two hours one of the temple windows blinked.

Magician Lang jumped to her feet and pulled out a magic sword. "Just as I thought!" she cried. "You can't fool me, Monkey! Your mouth is that door. You hoped to bite me as I walked in. Let's see what will happen if I smash those eyeball windows!"

"Oh, no you don't!" Monkey transformed back to himself, took his magic staff from behind his ear, and rushed upon Magician Lang.

How they fought! Great clouds of dust darkened the sky. Nine days and nine nights passed in furious battle.

High above them, on a cloud just outside the southern gate of Heaven, Goddess Guan-yin and Jade Emperor watched the struggle in silence. No one was winning. Magician Lang and Monkey were too evenly matched. At last Goddess Guan-yin decided she must act. She plucked a vase from her sleeve and threw it down to Earth.

Down, down it fell, growing in size until it landed right over Monkey! It held him so tightly he could not break free.

"Aha!" cried Jade Emperor. "Monkey is trapped at last!"

17

MONKEY IS CAPTURED

"**B**ring Monkey to Heaven," cried Jade Emperor when he saw that Monkey was trapped beneath the vase. He sent General Vaisravane and sixty thousand more soldiers to bind Monkey securely with magical ropes.

Everyone in the Heavenly Court cheered when Monkey—still tightly bound—was brought before Jade Emperor.

"Do you have anything to say for yourself, Monkey?" asked Jade Emperor.

"Yes," said Monkey. "I wish I had eyes on the top of my head."

"And why is that?"

"Then I would have seen the vase coming. If you hadn't cheated I would have won my battle against Magician Lang," Monkey complained.

Jade Emperor was outraged. "This

monkey is unrepentant!" he cried. "No punishment is too harsh for him."

And so, at the Emperor's orders, Monkey was tied to a pillar. Then heavenly soldiers attacked him with their shining knives and swords. But Monkey was as hard as a rock, and not a single hair on his body was hurt. "S-stop that," he giggled. "You're tickling me!"

Jade Emperor frowned. "Bring in Fire Star. *He* will know what to do."

Fire Star set up a blazing fire under Monkey. The flames were so hot that everyone stepped back. But Monkey just teased. "Emperor, how thoughtful! My toes were getting cold."

Jade Emperor scowled. "Bring in Thunder Spirit!"

Thunder Spirit began hurling huge bolts of lightning at Monkey. But Monkey only laughed, "Oh, good. I needed a massage!"

Monkey looked at Jade Emperor and shook his head. "Don't you know? After eating all those heavenly peaches I became immortal. I am indestructible!"

Jade Emperor uttered a piercing wail of desperate frustration. He hardly knew what to do next.

Goddess Guan-yin approached Jade Emperor. "Put him in a cauldron to burn for ninety-nine days. No one—mortal or immortal—could possibly survive that."

So Monkey was thrown into a cauldron. The lid was fastened, and a thousand guards were posted all around it. An enormous fire was lit, and such fierce flames leaped around the cauldron that after a while it could not be seen. Poor Monkey! It seemed impossible that even he could survive such treatment. All of Heaven waited with great impatience.

Ninety-nine days passed. Everyone in Heaven reassembled with the Emperor to view the cauldron. The blaze was finally put out, and the blackened cauldron set to cool. Finally nine soldiers removed the lid. All was quiet. No one wanted to look, and yet everyone leaned forward. . . .

The sound of a great yawn came from the depths of the cauldron. And out popped Monkey, rubbing his eyes! "Oh, what a nice

long warm nap I had," he said, and stretched his arms.

Jade Emperor was beside himself. "Destroy him!" he screamed.

At once the heavenly soldiers, General Vaisravane, his son Natha, the Kings of the Four Quarters, Thunder Spirit, and Fire Star attacked Monkey together. But Monkey took his magic staff from behind his ear and knocked over the cauldron. He struck at them recklessly, sending this one crying and that one running for cover.

Just when the fighting was at its fiercest, a deep voice thundered, "Stop! This fighting must stop immediately!"

Monkey looked up. A man with a wide forehead and extremely long earlobes was descending from a circle of light. All the generals and kings threw themselves down. Even Goddess Guan-yin and Jade Emperor bowed to him.

"I am in the middle of an important battle," Monkey complained. "Who are you to interfere?"

"I am Buddha," said the man. "And I

have come to end this dispute."

Of course, Monkey knew who Buddha was—the greatest being of the Western Paradise. He had learned all about Buddha from Master Subhodi. But so what? "How do you think you can stop me?" he sneered.

Buddha gazed down at him. At last he said softly, "Monkey, you have made a great deal of trouble."

"Me?" asked Monkey. "I've done nothing wrong. I'd merely like to replace Jade Emperor as the ruler of Heaven."

"You are ambitious." Buddha smiled. "What makes you worthy of such a position?"

Monkey thought for a second. "Well, I can transform into anything I like," he started. "I can leap one hundred and eight thousand leagues. I can live forever. Doesn't that make me truly magnificent?"

Buddha pondered this. "Very well, Monkey. I shall give you one chance to prove your worth. How does that sound?"

Monkey laughed. "I'm ready!"

18

WHAT FINALLY HAPPENED TO MONKEY KING

Great Buddha looked at Monkey and said, "You say that you are a good jumper. If you can jump out of the palm of my hand in one somersault, I shall let you rule Heaven. But if you fail, you must accept my punishment. Do you agree?"

Monkey could hardly believe his ears. "I just told him I could jump one hundred and eight thousand leagues!" he said to himself. "Perhaps great Buddha is hard of hearing. He must be foolish to make such a bet with me."

"Is this an honest deal?" Monkey asked out loud.

"Oh yes, we have many witnesses here," returned great Buddha with a smile. "Do you agree?"

"Of course I agree." Monkey shook with laughter.

Calmly, great Buddha held out his hand.

Monkey climbed into his palm. He stretched his legs and arms and wiggled all of his fingers and toes. Then, just as he had done so many years ago at the great waterfall, he crouched down, closed his eyes, took a deep breath, and leaped with all his might.

After a long moment he landed on his feet, quite certain he had gone at least one hundred and eight thousand leagues away from where he had started. Looking around, he saw an unfamiliar landscape, a boundless flat plain with five pillars soaring straight into the sky. Monkey walked around, looking for landmarks, but he couldn't find anything to tell him where he was.

"Hmm!" he said. "I must have jumped even farther than I thought! I guess this must be the very end of the world. But I suppose it would be a good idea to make a mark to show how far I came."

Monkey plucked a hair from his chest and cried, "Alalalatola!" The hair became a paintbrush. Monkey approached the pillar in the center and wrote *Magnificent Monkey King was here*. He thought for a second, then he urinated on the bottom of the pillar, grinning at his little trick.

Certain that he had won his bet with great Buddha, Monkey cloud-soared back to Heaven.

He jumped off the cloud and found he was standing again in great Buddha's hand. Monkey looked up in triumph. "All right, where is my throne?"

"Silly monkey," great Buddha said with a laugh. "You never left my palm."

"I knew you wouldn't believe me." Monkey grinned. "That's why I left my mark on one of the pillars at the end of the world."

"Ah, really?" Great Buddha couldn't stop smiling. "Look down."

Monkey looked down. At the base of one of great Buddha's fingers he saw his own handwriting. *Magnificent Monkey King was here.* Beneath it was a small puddle.

"It's—it's impossible!" Monkey sputtered. "I was at the end of the world. It must be a trick! Let me try again." He crouched down and was just about to make another

jump, but great Buddha quickly flipped his hand over and trapped Monkey in his grip. He then transformed his five fingers into a mountain range with five snow-capped ridges.

"To tell you the truth, Monkey," great Buddha said, "you will never be able to jump out of my hand, because my hand can expand without limit. My hand is everywhere—you just don't see it. Monkey, your mischief is done. You must stay here under this mountain until you learn to use your power wisely and usefully."

"Will I ever get out?" Monkey cried. He knew that this time he was truly trapped.

"That is up to you," said great Buddha. "When you have learned from your mistakes, I will release you. You have my word. And I promise I'll visit you in five hundred years to see what you have discovered."

"Five hundred years!" Monkey wailed from beneath the mountain.

But no one answered.

Monkey sighed, then lay back with his head resting on a rock. He closed his eyes.

After a few moments he broke into a grin.

"After all, five hundred years . . . that's not so much!" He tapped his chin thoughtfully. "It should give me just enough time to make a new plan!" And Monkey began to laugh.